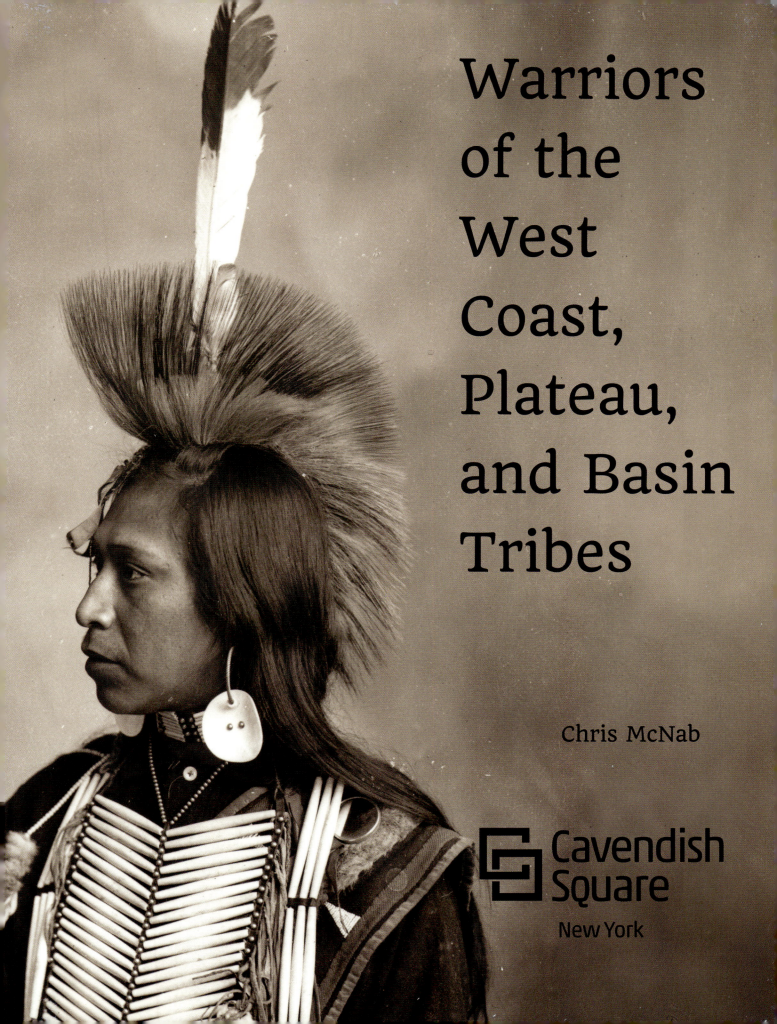

Warriors of the West Coast, Plateau, and Basin Tribes

Chris McNab

Cavendish Square
New York

This edition published in 2018 by Cavendish Square Publishing, LLC
243 5th Avenue, Suite 136, New York, NY 10016

© 2018 Amber Books Ltd.
All Rights Reserved.

Additional end matter copyright © 2018 by Cavendish Square Publishing, LLC

First Edition

No part of this publication may be reproduced, stored in a retrieval system, or transmitted in any form or by any means—electronic, mechanical, photocopying, recording, or otherwise—without the prior permission of the copyright owner. Request for permission should be addressed to Permissions, Cavendish Square Publishing, 243 5th Avenue, Suite 136, New York, NY 10016.
Tel (877) 980-4450; fax (877) 980-4454.

Website: cavendishsq.com

This publication represents the opinions and views of the author based on his or her personal experience, knowledge, and research. The information in this book serves as a general guide only. The author and publisher have used their best efforts in preparing this book and disclaim liability rising directly or indirectly from the use and application of this book.

All websites were available and accurate when this book was sent to press.

Cataloging-in-Publication Data

Names: McNab, Chris, author.
Title: Warriors of the West Coast, Plateau, and Basin Tribes / Chris McNab.
Description: New York : Cavendish Square Publishing, 2018. | Series: Native American warfare | Includes glossary and index. | Audience: Grades 6–10.
Identifiers: ISBN 9781502632982 (library bound) | ISBN 9781502633163 (ebook)
Subjects: LCSH: Indians of North America—Northwest, Pacific—Juvenile literature. | Indians of North America—Great Basin—Juvenile literature.
Classification: LCC E78.N77 M37 2018 | DDC 979.5004'97—dc23

Editorial Director: David McNamara
Editor: Erica Grove
Associate Art Director: Amy Greenan
Production Coordinator: Karol Szymczuk

The photographs in this book are used by permission and through the courtesy of: All maps and black-and-white line artworks produced by JB Illustrations © Amber Books; AKG Images: 47 & 75 (North Wind Picture Archives), 162 (North Wind Picture Archives); Alamy: 98tr (North Wind Picture Archives); Art Archive: 128/129 (William E. Weiss/Buffalo Bill Historical Center), 194 (Buffalo Bill Historical Center); Bridgeman Art Library: 88/89 (Peter Newark American Pictures), 104/105bl (Peter Newark American Pictures), 120 (Look & Learn), 133 (Peter Newark American Pictures), 135 & 151 (Look & Learn), 174 & 197 (Peter Newark American Pictures); Corbis: 19 & 20 (Bettmann), 22t (Werner Forman Archive), 32 (Robert Wagenhoffer), 39 (Marilyn Angel Wynn/Nativestock Pictures), 42, 55 (Medford Historical Society Collection), 56/57 (Historical Picture Archive), 58 (Historical Picture Archive), 62 (Nik Wheeler), 63, 64, 83 (Bettmann), 86 (Peter Harholdt), 112, 137, 143, 146, 152, 157, 158, 159, 160 (Bettmann), 161 (Poodles Rock), 165tr, 165b (Tria Giovan), 176, 184 (Bettmann), 192 (Werner Forman Archive), 206, 209, 210, 211, 214/215 (Bettmann) Dorling Kindersley: 105t (Geoff Brightling) Getty Images: 8 (Bridgeman Art Library), 11 (Roger Viollet), 15 (Joe Sohm/Visions of America), 25 (Time & Life Pictures), 29 (Marilyn Angel Wynn/Nativestock Pictures), 36, 48 & 74 (Bridgeman Art Library), 78br (Science & Society Picture Library), 79tr & 97 (Hulton Archive), 140 & 145 (Time & Life Pictures), 148 (SuperStock), 150 (Bridgeman Art Library), 170/171 (Hulton Archive), 177 (Hulton Archive), 178 (Marilyn Angel Wynn/Nativestock Pictures), 193 (Bridgeman Art Library), 204/205, 207 (Hulton Archive); iStockphoto: 153 (Duncan Walker); Library of Congress: 9, 12/13, 17, 27tr, 41, 45, 49, 50/51, 54, 59, 65tl, 65b, 70, 72tr, 76, 85tl, 85br, 98bl, 100, 106, 109tl, 111, 115, 117, 118, 119, 121, 125, 127tr, 130, 139, 141 (both), 144, 154/155, 156, 163, 164, 167, 168 & 169 (all), 180 (both), 183 & 183 (both), 185, 187, 188, 195, 198/199, 200, 208; Mary Evans Picture Library: 81, 147, 181; Photos.com: 78/79tl, 90, 91, 109b, 127b, 172, 175; Photoshot: 6/7 (World Illustrated), 22bl & 113 (UPPA), 179 (UPPA); Public Domain: 72bl, 122; TopFoto: 102/103 (Granger Collection), 138 & 191 (Granger Collection); U.S. Department of Defense: 213; Werner Forman Archive: 27b (Ohio State Museum), 202 (Anthropological Museum of Lomonosov, Moscow).

Printed in the United States of America

CONTENTS

Introduction	4
Chapter 1 Extermination in the West	6
Chapter 2 Weapons and Armor	19
Chapter 3 Fortifications and Battle Tactics	24
Chapter 4 The Pacific Northwest	31
Glossary	44
Further Reading	46
Index	48

INTRODUCTION

> "These Savages may, without injustice, be classed lower in the human scale than even the Esquimaux. Equally inanimate and filthy in habit, they do not possess that ingenuity and perseverance which their Northern neighbours can boast. Sullen and lazy, they only rouse themselves when pressed by want."
> – Turner (1836)

This judgment on the Indians of California, from the nineteenth-century lawyer George Turner, is not given here because of any belief in its accuracy. Its value for the historian, however, is a snapshot of the chilling mindset of the American settlers who, as we shall see, effectively implemented an extermination policy against the Native Americans of the west. The language used is almost indistinguishable from that applied by the Nazis to the Jews. Perhaps more than anywhere else, the clash of cultures between the Native Americans and the settlers was at its most extreme in the far west, which in turn had an impact on the manner of warfare practiced by the Indians of those territories.

This book takes in several Native American culture areas that together map out almost the whole of the western United States and a strip of western Canada. We are dealing with two (or perhaps three, depending on your perspective) distinct areas of Native American territory.

First, there is the westernmost strip of the United States, bordered by the Pacific Ocean and running from California up to Alaska. Bulging out from this strip towards the lands of the Plains Indians are the Plateau/Great Basin culture areas, the former belonging to the river-laced territories around the Columbia and Fraser Rivers, while the Great Basin refers to the arid and, in parts, mountainous land between the Rocky Mountains and the Sierra Nevada. More than 40 Native American tribes occupied these lands. The breadth of the peoples involved in this book means that a comprehensive history of every tribe involved is simply impossible. What we can achieve, however, is a look into how the native peoples of the western United States adjusted to and resisted the encroachment of the settlers from the east and the south, and how the Indians of these territories shared common styles of warfare as well as exhibiting some tribal peculiarities.

◀ Wary Indians watch the meeting of American explorer John Fremont and courier Archibald Gillespie, who delivers presidential orders telling Fremont to aid the American invasion of California, at this point (1846) still a part of Mexico.

CHAPTER 1

EXTERMINATION IN THE WEST

We start our analysis with the tribes of California and the Great Basin who faced encroachment into their territory from Spanish, Mexican and American settlers (see the feature box opposite for a list of major representative tribes in these areas).

Native American history in California stretches back at least 10,000 years. European intrusions, however, began in the sixteenth century with sporadic Russian, Spanish, Portuguese and English explorations. It was the Spanish, however, with their burgeoning empire to the south, who initially had the greatest impact upon the Californian Indians.

The Spanish

In the late eighteenth century, Spanish missionaries began to establish strings of missions along the Californian coastline. In customary fashion, the Spanish brought with them a terrible range of European diseases, which inflicted massive mortality upon many Native American tribes, achieving through biology what the soldiers could not achieve through force of arms. The word of God preached by the missionaries was heavily supported by the arms of man—Franciscans went out into the wilderness supported by intimidating bodies of heavily armed soldiers, just in case their scripture didn't carry enough force. Yet even those who converted to the new

▲ Early West Coast Indians practice their skills with bow and arrow. Although the range of the bow varied according to its construction, the warrior would be fairly confident of hitting a human-sized target at ranges of 98–164 feet (30–50m).

MAJOR GREAT BASIN TRIBES			MAJOR CALIFORNIA INDIAN TRIBES		
Bannock	Chemehuevi	Washoe	Kato	Maidu	Miwok
Mono	Northern Paiute	Panamint	Pomo	Chumash	Wintun
Shoshone	Southern Paiute	Ute	Yokuts	Yuki	Modoc

The position of the Great Basin and Californian Native American tribes meant that they experienced two settler cultures: that of the Spanish and Mexicans pushing up from the south, and that of the American settlers expanding their territories from the east.

religion could expect little comfort, as the French naval officer and explorer Jean François de Galaup, comte de La Pérouse, observed when he visited California in 1786, and saw the life of the neophytes:

"Every day they have seven hours of labor, two of prayers, and four or five on Sundays and feastdays, which are set apart for repose and Divine worship. Corporal punishment is inflicted upon the Indians of both sexes who fail in their religious exercises; and several offenses—for which in Europe the punishment is left to the hand of Divine justice—are punished here with irons. From the moment that a neophyte is baptized, it is the same as if he had taken perpetual vows; and, if he should escape from the mission, and take refuge among his relations in their Indian villages, he is summoned three times to return. If he refuses, the missionaries apply for the authority of the governor, who dispatches soldiers to drag him from the bosom of his family and take him back to the missions, where he is sentenced to receive so many lashes. These Indians are of so timid a character, that they never make any opposition to those who thus violate every human right ..."

– La Pérouse (1786)

La Pérouse was not entirely accurate in saying that the Californian Indians "never make any opposition," however. Native resistance to the muscular Spanish Christianity did take some active forms. The first mission established in California, at San Diego in 1769, was attacked by Kumeyaay Indians within weeks of its foundation, and it was entirely destroyed in

▲ A Jesuit priest attempts to convert Native Americans, under the coercive presence of Spanish soldiers. The effort to impose Christian religion did little but alienate the Indians and push them to military action.

◀ The Mojave Desert. Despite the austere nature of the terrain in this part of the world, several Indian tribes could comfortably operate here, including the Mohave and the Yavapai.

1775. Attacks widened to the Spanish population, especially when the Native Americans saw their lands trampled and their crops eaten by Spanish cattle. On July 17, 1781, for example, Kw'tsa'n and Mohave warriors attacked a Spanish settlement and killed 131 people. Other Indians who avoided conversion, or had escaped, banded together in guerrilla alliances in the San Joaquin Valley, making raids for horses and attacking the Spanish military and settlements.

In the end, it was the Mexicans rather than the Native Americans who overthrew the mission system in California. In 1823, following the Mexican War of Independence, Mexico took over the governance of California, and quashed clerical authority. For the Native Americans, the ascent of the Mexicans simply brought new levels of threat.

The Mexicans set about appropriating important tribal territories and, as a result, the Indian resistance grew more ferocious. The Miwoks and Yokuts in particular began a campaign of raiding Mexican settlements and trade routes; such was their effect that the Mexican government in the area ordered the establishment of forts in the interior to try to control them. Epidemics further crippled the Native American capacity to resist, and resulted in shocking reductions in population. In a period of around 70 years prior to the absorption of California into the United States, the population of the Californian Indians was reduced by at least 50 percent.

American Intervention

The Mexican–American War of 1846–48 once again transformed the fortunes of the California Indians. With the American victory, what had been the Mexican territory of Alta California was annexed by the United States, although at the time of the takeover the settler population of California was a mere 15,000 people. The demographics would change profoundly when gold was

Mohave Warrior

The Mohave Indians tended to dress with extreme simplicity—this warrior wears nothing more than a loincloth, small feather headdress and regular lines of ochre war paint. In battle, some Mohave were seen wearing a basic form of body armor, consisting of braided vines.

▲ **Alaska Territory, 1897. Five Chilkat porters pose with a miner and two oxen on the Dyea Trail, located at the head of the Chilkoot Trail. By this point in history, many of the West Coast Indians had been assimilated into settler culture.**

discovered in the hills of the Sierra Nevada in the late 1840s, resulting in the influx of more than 100,000 fortune-hunters in one year alone. The scene was set for a particularly brutal episode in the history of Indian–American relations. Tough-minded waves of settlers made the hunting and killing of Indians a near-sport, seeing the indigenous peoples as a threat to their gold prospecting and new way of life. The Indian tribes responded with the occasional murder, or with theft of livestock belonging to the settlers, but these actions incited truly disproportionate responses by the Americans. One settler, Dryden Lawson, recounted in 1860 that "… in 1856 the first expedition by the whites against the Indians was made … these expeditions were formed by gathering together a few white men whenever the Indians committed depredations on their stock; there were so many expeditions that I cannot recollect the number … we would kill on average fifty or sixty Indians on a trip … frequently we would have to turn out two or three times a week."

It has been estimated that 100,000 Indians were killed in California during the gold rush years. Genocide was sanctioned at the highest levels—in September 1859, the California governor John Weller actually commissioned an Indian-killer named Walter Jarboe to slaughter Indians indiscriminately—men, women and children. In the same year, the theft of a high-value stallion by Yuki Indians resulted in the massacre of 240 of their number in reprisal. Those not immediately killed were forced into the Round Valley Reservation established in 1854, where they were murdered, raped and assaulted with impunity.

SETTLER ATROCITIES

In 1860, the California legislature established the Joint Special Committee on the Mendocino Indian War (a settler–Indian conflict of 1859) to investigate alleged atrocities against Native Americans. The following extracts of the report illustrate the extreme nature of the violence against the Indians:

"Many of the most respectable citizens of Mendocino County have testified before your committee that they kill Indians, found in what they consider the hostile districts, whenever they lose cattle or horses; nor do they attempt to conceal or deny this fact. Those citizens do not admit, nor does it appear by the evidence, that it is or has been their practice or intention to kill women or children, although some have fallen in the indiscriminate attacks of the Indian *rancherias*. The testimony shows that in the recent authorized expedition against the Indians in said county, the women and children were taken to the reservations, and also establishes the fact that in the private expeditions this rule was not observed, but that in one instance, an expedition was marked by the most horrid atrocity; but in justice to the citizens of Mendocino County, your committee say that the mass of the settlers look upon such act with the utmost abhorrence ... Accounts are daily coming in from the counties on the Coast Range, of sickening atrocities and wholesale slaughters of great numbers of defenseless Indians in that region of country. Within the last four months, more Indians have been killed by our people than during the century of Spanish and Mexican domination..."

▲ Members of the Southern branch of the Paiute tribe, camped near Mendocino, 1876. They live in "wickiups" – huts of stick and brush fastened to poles made from willow trees.

Nor was the escalating war between the Indians and the settlers confined to California, but indeed it spread up the whole of the western United States.

Wider War

American settlers began to reach the Plateau/Great Basin area during the early 1800s. The area was rich ground for mining, particularly for gold, silver and copper. As in the case of California, the influx of settlers resulted in inevitable conflict with the native inhabitants, and the experience of the Shoshone Indians was typical.

The Shoshone inhabited the Great Basin around the Rocky Mountains, and their isolated existence suffered a rude shock when they encountered the Europeans during the 1840s. The voracious appetite of the settlers for the local wildlife led to serious hunger among the tribe. By the early 1860s, the Shoshone people had had enough and in 1862 they, along with the Bannock and Paiute tribes, launched a campaign against the settlers in California and Oregon.

The primary tactics of the Shoshone and their allies were raiding and ambushes, typical targets being miners walking woodland trails, wagon trains and stagecoaches. Eventually the Federal Government responded, pulling troops away from the demands of the American Civil War that had been raging for two years by this point. The main tool of enforcement was Colonel Patrick Connor's 1st California Cavalry, which had established a base at Fort Douglas near Salt Lake City. In January 1863, Connor set out into the freezing Midwestern winter in an operation to crush the

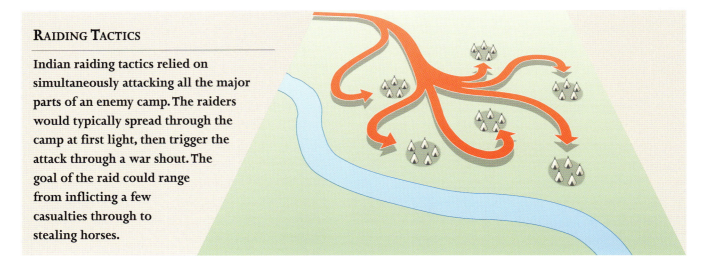

RAIDING TACTICS

Indian raiding tactics relied on simultaneously attacking all the major parts of an enemy camp. The raiders would typically spread through the camp at first light, then trigger the attack through a war shout. The goal of the raid could range from inflicting a few casualties through to stealing horses.

northwestern Shoshone, who were led by a warrior chief called Bear Hunter. The snowy conditions probably helped mask the approach of Connor's force, which discovered Bear Hunter's camp along the Bear River. Connor immediately launched a cavalry assault, which was initially repelled, but then the Americans managed to surround and overrun the Indian village, precipitating a horrible massacre of possibly as many as 400 of the Shoshone, the soldiers not discriminating between the victims, regardless of age and gender.

The defeat of Bear Hunter was a prelude of things to come. Connor won similar victories over other Shoshone groups and by the autumn the war was

▲ Bear River, the site of a major engagement between US soldiers and the Shoshone tribe in 1863. The US troops overran a Shoshone village, then massacred up to 400 people.

SHOSHONE TREATY, 1863

The following are Articles 1 and 2 of the treaty concluded between the United States of America and the Shoshone Indians on October 1, 1863:

ARTICLE 1
Peace and friendship shall be hereafter established and maintained between the Western Bands of the Shoshone nation and the people and government of the United States; and the said bands stipulate and agree that hostilities and all depredations upon the emigrant trains, the mail and telegraph lines, and upon the citizens of the United States within their country, shall cease.

ARTICLE 2
The several routes of travel through the Shoshonee country, now or hereafter used by white men, shall be forever free, and unobstructed by the said bands, for the use of the government of the United States, and of all emigrants and travellers under its authority and protection, without molestation or injury from them. And if depredations are at any time committed by bad men of their nation, the offenders shall be immediately taken and delivered up to the proper officers of the United States, to be punished as their offenses shall deserve; and the safety of all travellers passing peaceably over either of said routes is hereby guaranteed by said bands. Military posts may be established by the President of the United States along said routes or elsewhere in their country; and station houses may be erected and occupied at such points as may be necessary for the comfort and convenience of travellers or for mail or telegraph companies.

▲ A group of Ute Indians on the war path against the settlers, circa 1869. The Ute tribe was part of the Shoshone Nation, which ranged from Colorado and Utah south to New Mexico and Arizona.

essentially over. Another American victory was achieved by General George Crook, who during the "Snake War" (1866–68) took on the Northern Paiute Indians (known by the settlers as the Snake Indians) of the Pacific Northwest. Crook was one of the new breed of military commanders who recognized that conventional tactics were often unsuited to fighting Indians. For example, Kessel and Wooster point out that Crook "was an avid student of Indian tactics and often used them in his campaigns against hostile bands. During the course of the Snake War, he used Shoshone auxiliaries and traded his horses and wagons for pack mules. The mule was an animal well suited to negotiating difficult terrain, thus allowing the army better mobility" (Kessel and Wooster, 2005).

Crook's specially formed 23rd Infantry overwhelmed the Paiute through a combination of pursuits and minor battles. Crook's tactical policy served to wear down the Paiute over a prolonged period—he fought a total of 49 minor battles against the Indians before they finally relented and surrendered in July 1868.

The Modoc War and Final Defeat

The 1860s and the 1870s saw the final defeat of Indian armed resistance to the settlers in California. One of the final passionate stirrings of the Native American warrior spirit occurred in the Modoc War of 1872–73. Although the Modoc tribe of northern California and southwestern Oregon had a belligerent reputation, they were generally on reasonable terms with the local settlers. The Modocs

▲ General George Crook, the commander of US Army troops during the Snake War (1866–68). Crook had served with distinction in the US Civil War (1861–65) and was involved in the the Great Sioux War of 1876–77. He fought the Lakota at the Battle of the Rosebud.

▶ "Captain Jack," 1873. Actually named Kientopoos, Jack was best known for the killing of General Edward Canby during negotiations in the Modoc War (1872–73), an act for which he was eventually caught and hanged.

▲ A vivid portrayal of an action during the Modoc War of 1872–73. Difficult terrain was one of the Modoc's greatest assets during the conflict, not only providing hiding places for the Indians, but also protecting them from US firepower.

had signed a peace treaty with the settlers in 1864 after a period of violence, and had moved onto a reservation with the Klamath Indians, traditional enemies of the Modoc. However, a Modoc warrior leader, "Captain Jack" Kientopoos, caught the current during the rise of the Ghost Dance religion and rejected life on the reservation, leading a group of followers out from the reservation and back into the wilderness.

For the US authorities, Captain Jack's behavior was unacceptable, and US Army troops under Brigadier General Edward Canby finally tracked down the renegade band to the "Stronghold," a rocky lava bed at Tula Lake in northern California, which formed an almost impregnable natural barrier. Canby put down heavy artillery fire and made several assaults, but these resulted in little more than adding to the American casualty count (nine dead and 28 wounded on the first day). Worse was to come for the Americans. An attempt at diplomacy resulted in a meeting between Captain Jack and Canby on April 11, 1873, during which Jack proceeded to shoot and stab Canby to death. Jack and his men fled back to the Stronghold.

Modoc confidence was now running high. On April 26, a Modoc group headed by the warrior leader "Scarfaced Charley" ambushed an Army

Peace Policy and Subjugation

By the time the Modoc War ended in 1873, the Native Americans of the United States had already experienced four years of President Ulysses S. Grant's so-called "Peace Policy," an attempt to provide a lasting solution to conflict between the settlers and the Indians. In November 1869, Jacob D. Cox, Grant's Secretary of the Interior, wrote an annual report outlining the key objectives and intentions of the Peace Policy. His description of the effects of settlement,

▲ The Modoc finally surrender, emerging from the lava beds that were their refuge. By the time the war ended, less than 200 Modoc had survived, and they headed out to reservations in Indian Territory.

reconnaissance group of 85 men, including some Indian scouts. In the battle that followed, 25 of the soldiers were killed for few (possibly no) Indian losses. Yet although the Modoc seemed to have the tactical advantage, strategically their days were numbered. The Modoc band numbered only some 45–90 people, while the US poured in more troops. Evading such troops was exhausting and slowly Modoc morale and numbers withered. Finally, US troops under the command of the prominent Civil War veteran William Tecumseh Sherman forced the remaining Modoc warriors into either dispersal or surrender. Captain Jack was captured and hanged for Canby's murder in 1873.

▶ Paiute natives sit for the camera in this late-nineteenth-century photograph. Apart from bows, they have few weapons—the supplies of firearms to Western Indians was extremely limited.

spoken with pride rather than regret, are significant for this book as a whole:

"The completion of one of the great lines of railway to the Pacific coast has totally changed the conditions under which the civilized population of the country come in contact with the wild tribes. Instead of a slowly advancing tide of migration, making its gradual inroads upon the circumference of the great interior wilderness, the very center of the desert has been pierced. Every station upon the railway has become a nucleus for a civilized settlement, and a base from which lines of exploration for both mineral and agricultural wealth are pushed in every direction. Daily trains are carrying thousands of citizens and untold values of merchandise across the continent, and must be protected from the danger of having hostile tribes on either side of the route."

– Cox (1869)

▶ Mendocino County, California, 1890. Workers lay railroad track to support logging trains. The railroads not only brought more land-hungry settlers to the west, but also resulted in the deforestation of Native American lands.

Cox's description of expanding US settlement would make sobering reading to those contemporary Native Americans who could understand the language. The "slowly advancing tide of migration" has an inexhaustible feel, and the development of the railway makes it clear that even the remotest areas would come under American jurisdiction. Cox continued his document by reflecting on the need to control the Native American population for the protection of the settlers. He explained how the government had two principal aims:

"First, the location of the Indians upon fixed reservations, so that the pioneers and settlers may be freed from the terrors of wandering hostile tribes; and, second, an earnest effort at their civilization, so that they may themselves be elevated in the scale of humanity, and our obligation to them as fellow-men be discharged."

– Cox (1869)

Just 20 years after Cox made this declaration, the objectives of the Peace Policy were essentially complete. During the 1890s, the frontier was declared officially "closed," all of the United States having been explored apart from some pockets of Alaska. The Indian tribes were largely confined to demoralizing reservations or restricted areas. The settler conquest of the Native American peoples was now complete, but we will now look at how the Indians of the west managed to sustain some level of military resistance even against the tide of inevitable defeat.

CHAPTER 2

Weapons and Armor

Regarding traditional weaponry, the Western Indians used the familiar range of spear, club and missile arms with some regional differences. For example, Indian tribes of California and the Great Basin/Plateau regions were known for firing poisoned arrows from their bows, the poisons having been developed over the centuries for hunting game. The poisons used a mixture of ingredients, and carried with them varying degrees of lethality. Sometimes the poisons were extracted from plants such as (in the case of California Indians) the Giant Horsetail Fern, American Pepper Plant or Turkey Mullen. In other cases, concoctions were brewed from animal poisons or the process of putrefaction. The Western Mono and the Southeastern Yavapai made particularly aggressive poisons by stuffing a deer's liver with the toxic parts of rattlesnakes and spiders then either cooking it slowly over a fire or leaving it out in the sun to putrefy. When the time was right, the Indian warriors would dip the tips of their spears and arrows in the caustic organ, then store them in special quivers or holders out of the reach of children. The efficacy of this poison was impressive but slow-working—typically it would take an injured deer about 24 hours to drop dead from the effects. Some accounts refer to settler soldiers dying two days after receiving little more than a minor scratch from such a poisoned arrow.

Other poisons made by the California Indians would not disgrace the pages of a manual on witchcraft. David E. Jones, author of *Poison Arrows: North American Indian Hunting and Warfare* describes one poison made by the Atsugewi tribe that consisted of:

▲ A Mohave native with bow and arrows. A classic Western Indian bow type was a yew bow backed with a very thin layer of sinew, to increase the reflex power when the bow was released. Juniper, hickory and ash were also used.

"... a deer pancreas, the gall of a coyote, the air bladder of a fish, red paint, and rattlesnake teeth. The concoction was then mixed in a mortar and permitted to rot before being applied to the arrow or spear points. Another Atsugewi informant told of a method of creating poison in which rattlesnake heads and chopped-up roots of wild parsnip were put in a skin with a handful of arrow points, and allowed to rot before attaching them to arrows."

– Jones (2007)

Rattlesnake and plant poisons were found in Native American warfare throughout the western United States, although sometimes a poison could simply involve dipping the point of a spear or arrow in rotted meat or excrement, thereby inducing tetanus in the victims.

Bows

Along the western coastline, self-bows made of yew, juniper, hickory or ash were the most common style, these typically ranging in length from 36–56 inches (91–142cm), although bows made at the extreme top end of the scale tended to be rarer and used only for long-range hunting and warfare. Arrow shafts were made from witch hazel, dogwood, viburnum and reed, and the points from obsidian, flint or steel.

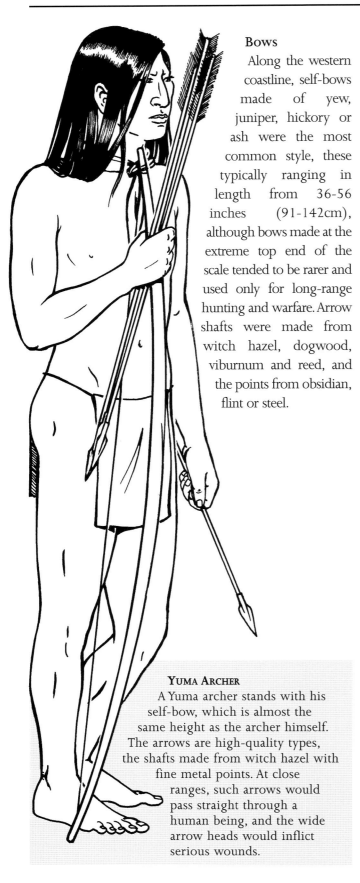

YUMA ARCHER
A Yuma archer stands with his self-bow, which is almost the same height as the archer himself. The arrows are high-quality types, the shafts made from witch hazel with fine metal points. At close ranges, such arrows would pass straight through a human being, and the wide arrow heads would inflict serious wounds.

In the Rocky Mountains range, and in the Great Basin/Plateau territories, bows were often made from yew wood imported from further west, but often the problems of sourcing good bow woods in these regions meant that the tribes constructed composite bows using the horns of sheep or buffalo. One interesting feature seen in Western bows is a type of "silencer." A major constituent part of the Western Indian diet was deer, a creature easily frightened by the slightest noise. When hunting deer, it was often found that the animal would flinch and start at the sound of a bow being released, and move before the flying arrow could strike it.

To deaden this noise, special dampers made from soft mink or otter fur were tied around the tip of the bow, nestling around the point where the bowstring attached to the bow. When the bow was fired, these dampers suppressed the "twang" of the string, eliminating the prior warning to the prey. These dampers also proved useful in subsequent conflict with the settlers.

While accuracy of fire was rarely a problem for the Native Americans, having adequate supplies of arrows was another matter. Unlike mass-produced ammunition, arrows required investment of time and skill to produce, and hours or days of careful arrow manufacture could be expended in minutes of combat. Such is evident in an account by Sigismundo Taraval, a Jesuit missionary who worked in Baja California during the 1730s and 1740s, and often experienced the hostility of the Native Americans to his religious objectives. In this extract from his *Indian Uprising in Lower California, 1734–1737*, Taraval describes an attack by local Indians on his group of missionaries, soldiers and allied Indians:

"From the start they hurled endless stones and arrows. Our men, in turn, fired only spasmodically, since the natives were so well situated that we could inflict but little damage. In fact, the natives who were hiding were so well concealed that they could be seen only at the instant when they shot arrows, for afterwards they immediately crouched down …

The fight lasted as long as the arrows lasted. I had warned our Indians not to shoot, since the sooner the enemy exhausted their arrows, the sooner would the attack, danger, and anxiety be over. This was exactly what happened, for within one-half hour the rebels had run out of arrows, although our men had not returned their fire, and so they were forced to withdraw precipitately."
— *Taraval (1967)*

It is impossible to tell in this extract whether the Indian rebels were using string dampers or not, but it certainly seems that the fact that they could only be identified when standing to fire meant that their practice of cover and concealment was excellent. Unlike many other Indian battles however, fire discipline seems less strict, especially as the enemy was not returning fire. The attack faltered because the men simply ran out of ammunition and were unable to prosecute their attack any further. It is hard to imagine Geronimo, for example, making such a mistake.

Ammunition supply was not only a problem in relation to arrows. The Western Indians did have firearms, but as they were mainly captured from the settlers, there was no standardization in

▲ Paiute Indians sit in their native terrain with bows and arrows. Between 1860 and 1868, the Paiute fought a bitter war with the American settlers. In one action in 1860, the Paiute killed some 70 US Army soldiers, trapped in an ambush along a narrow trail.

ammunition types. During the Battle of Bear River (see above), one of the reasons behind the Shoshone defeat was that they ran out of musket balls. During the battle some Indians were observed attempting to

▲ A Hupa Indian waits patiently for a fish to appear. The Hupa lived in the Hupa Valley, California, and by the early nineteenth century their numbers had dropped to less than 1000 individuals.

cast new shot, and after the battle the dead were even found still clutching their bullet molds.

Spears, Blades and Clubs

In addition to bows, the Western Indians carried an age-old assortment of spears, clubs and blades. The oldest traditional type of blade weapon was the obsidian knife. The edge of the obsidian was knapped with a piece of antler or another stone until it took an extremely sharp edge.

Although an obsidian blade was easily damaged, until the introduction of metal blades it gave similar cutting capability, and hence was useful in both war and for hunting. It also, according to this US Government report of 1806, could have ceremonial and spiritual significance.

Obsidian was used widely for all manner of weapons, including arrowheads, but its properties as a weapon material were questionable. On the one hand, it could undoubtedly achieve a very sharp edge and so made a lethal cutting tool. On the other hand, it was extremely brittle and could shatter easily. Ironically, sometimes this brittle quality was a positive advantage—an obsidian knife or arrowhead stuck in a victim might shatter into several shards, none of which could easily be removed.

In terms of clubs, the most popular varieties were simply knobbed sticks made from suitable hardwoods. The Western Indians also used throwing sticks in hunting and in warfare. These were largely the same as the regular clubs but might be made from heavier woods, such as mahogany, to ensure that they brought down their targets on impact.

> "So, too, the Yurok and Hupa Indians of California, as well as some of the tribes of Oregon, have very large spearheads or knives, which are not designed for use, but only to be produced on the occasion of a great dance. The larger weapons are wrapped in skin to protect the hand; the smaller ones are glued to a handle. Some are said to be 15 inches [38cm] long. The Oregon Indians believed the possession of a large obsidian knife brought long life and prosperity to the tribe owning it."
> – US Government (1806)

CHAPTER 3

FORTIFICATIONS AND BATTLE TACTICS

The fortification situation in the west was varied, and depended largely upon the terrain and the type of tribe. In the California area, Native American fortifications were actually relatively rare, mainly on account of the high mobility involved with the hunter-gatherer lifestyle. A select few Californian tribes built simple fortifications consisting of trenches and lodges dug into the earth and covered with earth or plant materials.

Fortification building in the Plateau/Basin regions was similarly basic, typically a combination of trenches working in combination with protective breastworks. *Ad hoc* fortifications and barricades could be constructed in sudden emergencies, using whatever materials and landscape features were in the vicinity. David Jones quotes explorer E.M. Harmon, who in the mid-1940s wrote about a Ute fortification he discovered in Colorado. Local people informed Harman that it had originally been built when a Ute hunting party, which included women and children, was suddenly faced with a sizeable force of Cheyenne and Arapaho raiders. Apparently the construction was of such strength that the much larger group of raiders was unable to penetrate it through direct attack, and eventually retreated. Harmon describes the fortification as follows:

"On the crest of a timbered knoll sloping down to the Fraser River a short distance from the town of Granby, there is what apparently must have been a fort at some time. The side of the knoll away from the river is supported by a ledge of sandstone, forming a perpendicular wall or cliff some fifty or sixty feet [15–18m] in height, from the top of which the crescent-shaped barricade, composed of rocks and rotted logs, enclosed a clear space of less than half an acre [0.2ha] in extent."

– Harmon (1945)

These types of improvised fortifications were admirable works of defenses to build while actually under attack. Yet as the Indians clashed increasingly with the settlers rather than one another, any form of static defensive structure became inadvisable, as it would merely serve to contain the Indians for the firepower of the Europeans.

In fact, on the whole, the supply of firearms to Native Americans in the west was more restricted than

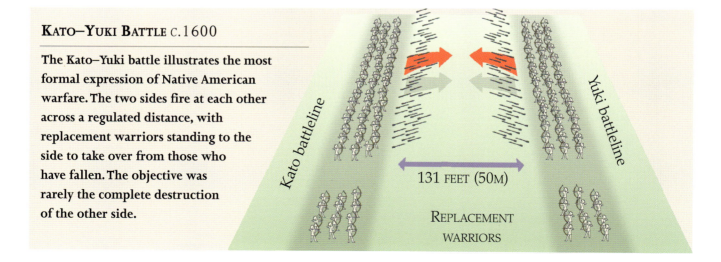

KATO–YUKI BATTLE C.1600

The Kato–Yuki battle illustrates the most formal expression of Native American warfare. The two sides fire at each other across a regulated distance, with replacement warriors standing to the side to take over from those who have fallen. The objective was rarely the complete destruction of the other side.

was the case further east, particularly in the California area during its "extermination phase," when any trade in firearms to the Indians was strictly prohibited. The Indians would have to fall back on their native hunting skills if they were to win small victories in a much larger war.

Tactics

Compared to the Native Americans of the opposite coastal zone, the populations of Western Indians, particularly in the California area, were often small. A limited population base, at least in the pre-contact phase of their existence, tended to produce extremely formalized styles of combat, structured so as to produce light casualties that didn't threaten the integrity of a tribe. Inter-tribal conflict was generally expressed through the prearranged "standing line" tactics that we have seen in other chapters.

Formal Warfare

A good example of this type of warfare is seen in the sixteenth century in a clash between the Kato and Yuki tribes of northern California, who fought a series of battles over rights to access an obsidian mining site. Rights over locations where obsidian was in plentiful supply could be fiercely contested, and brought the Yuki and Kato into conflict on several occasions. In one incident, a Kato woman was killed and beheaded by Yuki warriors.

Such was not an unusual fate in clashes between the tribes—the Kato also practiced beheading, the heads of the defeated being taken back to the village where they were boiled and the entire scalp removed as a trophy of battle. On this occasion, the killing was a catalyst for a formal battle, to which the Kato invited the Yuki via messengers.

A location for the fight was agreed, and a smoke signal raised on the day of battle to indicate the time.

▲ Indian warriors in battle count coup on horseback. Touching the enemy with a coup stick could signify bravery as much as the act of killing an enemy in battle and testified to the swift horsemanship of the warrior.

The subsequent engagement was strictly controlled, with lines of warriors advancing to within bowshot of one another and shooting showers of arrows at the enemy ranks. Observers stood to one side and periodic pauses in the action gave the tribal chiefs an opportunity to make a count of the dead and wounded. The war was played out in this fashion over several separate days, with gaps of as much as 10 days between each engagement, only coming to a close when one side had reached a defined level of casualties that effectively classified it as the loser in the overall battle.

An interesting outcome of the battle, however, was that the side that "won" the war was actually then obliged to pay compensation to the losers for the destruction of persons or property. Jones notes that "this custom created a dichotomous situation in which the military winners often became the economic losers" (Jones, 2004).

Such an arrangement probably had a limiting effect on the number of conflicts fought between the Native

an enemy during a battle then making an escape, this act bringing the warrior honor and reputation for bravery amongst his peers and tribe, as well as illustrating daring, speed and ingenuity.

Note that counting coup did not actually involve harming the enemy warrior; he was simply touched with the hand or with a special coup stick designed for the purpose. Coup sticks were extensively adorned with feathers, fur, scalps, bones and other declaration, and had magical connotations akin to those of a wand. When a warrior returned from battle, he would tap the coup stick against a special pole stuck in the ground in the village, the noise marking his victory. There was also some curious etiquette about counting coup, such as that if the warrior touched by the coup-seeking Indian was subsequently killed by another person, the honor of the coup still went to the person who had first counted coup, not to him who had done the killing. Counting coup is a strange practice to Western military eyes, but probably also had an additional limiting effect on the casualty counts of inter-tribal conflicts.

Guerrilla Warfare

These traditional, formalized styles of warfare naturally had little currency once the Indians came into conflict with the settlers, who placed no value on ostentatious displays of bravery in their extermination policies. Here the Native American tribes of the west had to rely more on guerrilla tactics if they were to survive, let alone win battles.

We have already become familiar with the Indian techniques of evasion, maneuver, raiding and ambush in previous chapters, and in the west these also formed the cornerstones of their resistance to the settlers. As with everything, hunting techniques informed the strategies of warfare, particularly in terms of cover, concealment and movement.

Rarely did the Indians of the west actually seek pitched battles with conventional forces. Rather, they preferred to wear away at units with frequent minor attacks, or target exposed and vulnerable settler communities rather than "hard" military objectives. Contrary to how the settlers perceived attacks on civilians, they were rarely conducted because of

▲ A Blackfoot counting coup stick. Coup sticks varied in length from around 12 inches (30 cm) up to 30 inches (76 cm), but generally speaking the shorter the stick, the greater its testimony to the bravery of the user.

American tribes, as even victory brought penalties and in hard times such must have been a strong disincentive to fight.

Counting Coup

One aspect of Native American warfare that we have not so far considered is the practice of "counting coup." This is most commonly associated with the Plains Indians, although it was actually practiced to various degrees amongst tribes throughout North America, particularly in the Great Basin/Plateau regions. Counting coup basically involved touching

Hunting Techniques

Josiah Conder, a geographer who travelled through American territory in the first half of the nineteenth century, made some observations of the ingenuity displayed by the Indians during hunting:

"The Indians make use, however, of another very ingenious artifice to approach the stags, and kill them. They cut off the head of a *venado*, the branches of which are very long; and they empty the neck, and place it on their own head. Masked in this manner, and armed also with bows and arrows, they conceal themselves in the brushwood, or among the high and thick herbage. By imitating the motion of a stag when it feeds, they draw round them the flock, which become the victims of the deception. This extraordinary hunt was seen by M. Costanzo on the coast of the channel of Santa Barbara; and it was seen twenty-four years afterwards, in the savannas in the neighborhood of Monterey, by the officers embarked in the *galetas* Sutil and Mexicana."

– Conder (1830)

▲ A Native American hunting moose in the Northwestern territory, circa 1880. Note the use of rudimentary wooden skis to get close to the animal to deliver a spear blow.

cowardice or laziness. Settlers, whether in uniform or not, represented a threat to the Indian way of life. While the Indians could never hope to eliminate the settlers from North America, they could attempt to dissuade them from passing through or exploiting their tribal lands. Unfortunately, the excesses that resulted from such a strategy, often provided the excuse for the settlers to dehumanize the Indians.

▲ A settler outpost in the Western United States in the second half of the nineteenth century. Such outposts, and the trail routes stretching off into the distance, were common targets for Native American attacks.

Use of Terror

One example of an Indian terror attack occurred in 1859 on the Oregon Trail near Fort Hall, Idaho. One of the survivors of what became known as the Late Massacre at Fort Hall, Milton J. Harrington, made a statement about what occurred to the *Desert News*:

"Our company numbered 19 persons 6 men 3 women and 10 children between 1 and 10 years old. Some of the company was from Michigan and the others from Buchanan County, Iowa. At the last crossing of the Sweet Water, we were advised to travel on Lander's Cuttoff being told that that route was nearer, better feed, and safe from Indian depredations.

Our journey was prosperous until the night of the 2nd when we were selecting our place for camping and were making our camp fires. We were startled at the report of a gun, followed immediately by a number of others. We soon ascertained that our rear wagons, which had not yet arrived in camp, were attacked by the Indians. A boy about 10 years old came running to us and said the Indians had killed his father and were killing all the rest. In a moment's time we were surrounded by the savages, whose hideous yells and constant cracking of their rifles at this moment rendered the scene too horrid for description. Those of us who survived made our escape by taking refuge in some rushes and willows on the bank of the Portneuf where we remained during the night. Next day we started on our journey on foot and after traveling three days on scant rations we came to Lieut. Livingston's company of dragoons who were escorting a party to Fort Walla Walla, Oregon."

The account illustrates several key points about Indian guerrilla warfare. First, it is evident that the presence of Indians influenced the common routes of travel taken by the settlers, as is apparent from the discussion about their route being "safe from Indian depredations" (implying that many others were not). Second, the Indian attack initially targets the rear of the passing column, a softer opportunity than the head of the column, which benefited from the fact that all eyes faced forward. The full force of the attack is unleashed with tempo and aggression, and only flight and hiding saves the surviving settlers from a gruesome fate. Just how gruesome this could be is described in the rest of Harrington's account:

FORTIFICATIONS AND BATTLE TACTICS

"After informing the command of our distress, Livingston sent a detachment of nine men with one of our company to pilot them to the place of the massacre. Upon their arrival, they found the dead bodies of 5 persons on the ground out of the 8 that were missing. The dead were horribly mangled and scalped. One little girl five-years-old, had both her legs cut off at the knees. Her ears were also cut off and her eyes were dug out from their sockets and, to all appearances, the girl after having her legs cut off had been compelled to walk on the stumps for the sole purpose of gratifying the hellish propensity of savage barbarity."

— *Desert News* (1859)

There is good reason not to accept accounts such as this at face value. Stories of Indian atrocities were frequently embellished by the American press, often under the official encouragement of the authorities who wanted to fire up the local population in support

▲ A Modoc warrior lifts up the freshly cut scalp from his latest victim. As well as taking scalps, the Western Indians would also take the weapons from the fallen enemy, who were one of their major sources of firearms.

of their aggressive anti-Indian policies. There were indeed many well-documented accounts of Indian "barbarity," but many of these related to the practice of scalping or the torture of prisoners. Although undoubtedly horrifying, battlefield mutilation and the torture of prisoners often had deeper spiritual significance for the Native Americans. As we have seen, scalping produced a physical token of bravery, while some tribes practiced beheading as a method of acquiring trophies of war. Regarding the torture of prisoners, this activity was not done without purpose. Amongst some tribes, torture was used almost as a means for gaining respect for enemies—the braver the prisoner was while being tortured, the greater the respect the tribe had for him. This could even help improve his chances of his survival.

Women and children were undoubtedly killed by Native American warriors, but the account of the girl having to walk on severed legs is questionable. Often children were simply dispatched with a blow from a club, the thinking being that they couldn't be left alive as they would be an extra mouth to feed—adopting them would place a strain on the resources of the tribe. Despite this, there were many instances where settler children were indeed adopted into Indian society. Yet whether the account of the atrocities were true or not, they had the desired effect on the settlers—a virulent hatred of the American Indians that enabled extermination policies to thrive.

Of course, civilian settlers were not the only targets of Indian guerrilla warfare. During the Paiute War of 1860, the Nevada Paiute often took on conventional US forces in ambush actions. The war began in a typically sordid fashion, after the rape of two Paiute girls led the Indians in a revenge attack on the Williams Station trading post which killed five settlers. A body of just over 100 settler volunteers were gathered to resolve the situation, commanded by Major William Ormsby. Inexperience shone through from the very beginning of the operation when, on May 12, a group of mounted soldiers galloped after a group of fleeing Paiute. The soldiers had little idea that they were falling into a carefully laid ambush until Indian arrows and bullets began to scythe through their ranks. After an about-turn, the volunteer soldiers became trapped along the trail, where subsequent Paiute ambushes whittled down their numbers even further. By the time the remainder of the column found safety, 42 soldiers were dead and 30 missing.

This pattern of attrition and counter-attrition defined much of the warfare in the west, although in the end, Native American tribes could not resist the overwhelming powers of demographics, disease and the increasing counter-insurgency skills of many US Army commanders. The result was that the odds were so stacked against them that they could not push home any advantage they might have gained.

TLINGIT TOTEM POLE
Totem poles were specific to the tribes of the Northwest Pacific Coast and were typically carved from solid cedar tree trunks. Monumental carving probably dates back centuries in Native American culture, but by the end of the nineteenth century the practice was in steep decline.

CHAPTER 4

The Pacific Northwest

The Native Americans of the Pacific Northwest (the territory between northern California and southern Alaska) had a very different culture from those in California or living in the Plateau/Basin territories. Tribes such as the Haida, Tlingit and Chinook generally lived in large, stable and static communities, much of their food coming from either saltwater or freshwater sources. Battles between Northwest tribes were fought for largely the same reasons as they were fought anywhere. Like the Indians further south, the Northwestern Native Americans were subject to encroaching colonization from the sixteenth century onwards, not only from Western Europe but also from

▲ The Lewis and Clark Expeditions confront a canoe of Native American warriors. Generally, Lewis and Clark established good relations with Indians they met, without whom the expedition would have starved.

Russia, and during the nineteenth century the process of subjection was completed through a familiar pattern of assimilation, violence and disease.

Seaborne Warfare

Coastal living had a dramatic effect on the Northwestern Indian style of warfare. Ambushes and raids were delivered directly from canoes, rather like the Vikings preying on the coastline of Western Europe. Amphibious actions could be very substantial indeed—David Jones notes that the Kwakwaka'wakw tribe "delivered hundreds of men to a battle, or more likely ambush, in 50- to 70-foot [15–21m] canoes, each carrying thirty to fifty men. The Northwest Coast people often battled on open water in such canoes."

The explorer Ross Cox, in his 1832 book *Adventures on the Columbia River*, described the process by which the Chinook Indians (who lived in British Columbia and Washington State) fought with a neighboring tribe. Cox first sets the scene:

TLINGIT CANOE
Being used for coastal travel as well as on inland waters, Tlingit canoes were very substantial affairs, often capable of holding a dozen men. They were dug-out canoes, produced by hollowing out large cedar and spruce logs. Some of the largest specimens of Northwestern Native American canoes stretched up to 60 feet (18m) in length.

▲ A Yurok Indian canoe glides down a river. Note that the construction gives the vessel a particularly shallow draft, ideal for navigating inland rivers. Being dug-out canoes, these craft were very durable, hence they might also be used as barricades from behind which the warriors could fire arrows and throw spears.

"The great mass of the American Indians, in their warlike encounters, fall suddenly on their enemies, and taking them unprepared, massacre or capture men, women, and children. The plan adopted by the Chinooks forms an honorable exception to this system. Having once determined on hostilities, they give notice to the enemy of the day on which they intend to make the attack: and having previously engaged as auxiliaries a number of young men whom they pay for that purpose, they embark in their canoes

▲ A Spokane hunting party, armed with clubs, knives, bow and arrows and a percussion cap rifle. Firearms never entirely replaced bows, although bow use did decline dramatically with the use of unitary cartridge guns.

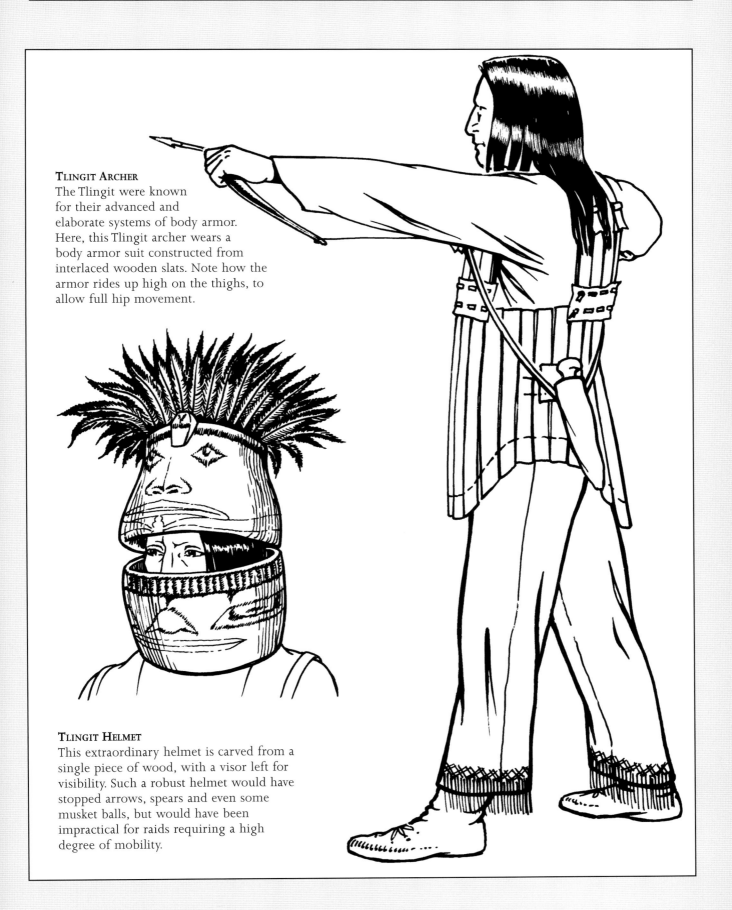

TLINGIT ARCHER
The Tlingit were known for their advanced and elaborate systems of body armor. Here, this Tlingit archer wears a body armor suit constructed from interlaced wooden slats. Note how the armor rides up high on the thighs, to allow full hip movement.

TLINGIT HELMET
This extraordinary helmet is carved from a single piece of wood, with a visor left for visibility. Such a robust helmet would have stopped arrows, spears and even some musket balls, but would have been impractical for raids requiring a high degree of mobility.

for the scene of action. Several of their women accompany them on these expeditions, and assist in working the canoes."

— Cox (1832)

Much like the formalized straight-line battles described earlier, the Chinook Indians make an agreement with the enemy regarding the time and place of the battle. The critical difference comes in the form of deployment. Using canoes, the Chinook row the warriors into battle, taking them directly to the enemy's coastal settlement. Once they arrive, however, the two parties then appear to make concerted efforts to avoid a physical clash.

"On arriving at the enemy's village they enter into a parley, and endeavor by negotiation to terminate the quarrel amicably. Sometimes a third party, who preserves a strict neutrality, undertakes the office of mediator; but should their joint efforts fail in procuring redress, they immediately prepare for action. Should the day be far advanced, the combat is deferred, by mutual consent, till the following morning; and they pass the intervening night in frightful yells, and making use of abusive and insulting language to each other. They generally fight from their canoes, which they take care to incline to one side, presenting the higher flank to the enemy; and in this position, with their bodies quite bent, the battle commences. Owing to the cover of their canoes, and their impenetrable armor, it is seldom bloody; and as soon as one or two men fall, the party to whom they belonged acknowledge themselves vanquished, and the combat ceases. If the assailants be unsuccessful, they return without redress; but if conquerors, they receive various presents from the vanquished party in addition to their original demand. The women and children are always sent away before the engagement commences."

— Cox (1832)

Several elements of this engagement are particularly fascinating when compared to the other actions studied in this book. From the fact that the warriors "generally fight from their canoes," it is obvious that the combat takes place close to the shoreline, the Indians simply pulling their canoes up onto the shore then placing them on their sides as defensive. As with so many other formal combats, the action is very much focused on casualty limitation, not least because the warriors appear to be heavily armored. In fact, the Northwest Indians invested more in the development and wearing of body armor than most other Native American groups.

Northwestern Body Armor

The early accounts of settlers in the Northwestern region reveal very sophisticated types of armor indeed. Tlingit warriors observed in the late eighteenth century, for example, wore entire suits made from wooden slats stitched together with thick cord or rawhide. This flexible system sometimes protected the warrior from his neck to his ankles, and included arm protection also, while the entire head was encased in a solid wood helmet—vision came via a thin eye-slit in the front. Thus protected, the Tlingit would have been hard targets to wound or kill, not least because the wooden armor was worn over the top of a thick leather coat. In fact, stories from around this period state that the Tlingit armor was even capable of stopping a musket ball at relatively close range. A Russian account of 1792 observed that Russian troops engaging the Tlingit fired directly at the helmets to achieve penetration.

The suits were designed to provide for a reasonable degree of movement. Haida armor was similar to that of the Tlingit, and while slats were used for the front and back of the armor, smaller wooden rods were employed at the sides, where they allowed for the body's flexing and bending. Other Northwestern tribes, such as the Tsimshian, created body armor from a combination of layers of elk hide and wooden rods.

▲ A section of a highly decorated Tlingit breastplate, made from deerskin. Although the physical protection afforded by such "armor" was limited, the decorations were also supposed to give some spiritual protection.

Fortifications

The protective mentality of the Northwest Indians is also evident in their strong systems of fortification. The building of fortifications in the Northwest stretches back at least 1500 years, and had developed into a sophisticated art by the time of settler expansion from the sixteenth century. Typically, a fortification was built in a naturally strong position, such as at the summit of a cliff or in elevated, inaccessible and rocky location. Fortifications also took advantage of rivers, which could provide protection for an exposed flank.

The layout of the fortification varied from tribe to tribe, but typically revolved around arrangements of wooden palisades, ditches (both dry and wet) and defensive measures such as spiked branches set in the ground or projecting from the top of the palisades. Palisades might be arranged in single or double rings, and inside the fortification the Indians frequently erected observation/fighting platforms, from which they could scan the surrounding countryside for threats as well as launch spears and arrows at attackers below. The ladders leading up to such platforms could be quickly pulled up if an enemy managed to penetrate the outer defenses and enter the fortification.

The scale of the Northwestern fortifications could be impressive. In one fort constructed by the Quinault tribe of coastal Oregon, a total of some 1800 people lived inside a palisaded enclosure built from 16 feet (5m) high cedar and cottonwood beams. A running

TLINGIT FORT
This Tlingit fort consists of wood-framed habitations surrounded by a buttressed perimeter wall. In some fortifications, the outer wall would also be surrounded by ditch defensive works, or spiked branches set in the ground as obstructions to attackers. Such fortifications required considerable investment in time and materials to construct, in contrast to the impermanent villages of the nomadic Indian tribes.

walkway set just below the top of the palisade acted as a 360-degree fighting platform.

The Battle of Sitka Sound

One of the most dramatic clashes between the fortified Northwest Indians and the settlers was that which occurred at Sitka Sound, southern Alaska, in 1804 between the Tlingit and the Russians of the Russian–American Company and the Imperial Russian Navy. Animosity between the Tlingit and the Russians stretched back some way. The Russian–American Company had established an outpost just to the north of the Tlingit's hilltop fortification at Sitka, and initial good relations deteriorated as the two peoples clashed culturally and over natural resources. On June 20, 1802, increasing friction came to a head when a large group of Tlingit warriors attacked the Russian outpost, aided by the fact that Western European settlers, who were equally eager to see the back of the Russians, had provided the Tlingit with modern firearms and cannon. The attack was overwhelming, and 150 of the inhabitants of the outpost (mostly Russian-allied Aleut Indians) were massacred and all the buildings burnt and destroyed.

Understanding full well that Russian reprisals would follow this successful but bloody assault, the Tlingit chose to rebuild their fortification, but this time on a much more substantial basis. Urey Lisyansky, a Russian naval officer who was involved in the impending battle at Sitka, described the resulting construction, set between the sea to its front and woodland to its rear:

"THE FORT WAS AN IRREGULAR SQUARE, ITS LONGEST SIDE LOOKING TOWARDS THE SEA. IT WAS CONSTRUCTED OF WOOD, SO THICK AND STRONG, THAT THE SHOT FROM MY GUNS COULD NOT PENETRATE IT AT THE SHORT DISTANCE OF A CABLE'S LENGTH. ... IT HAD A DOOR ... AND TWO HOLES ... FOR CANNON IN THE SIDE FACING THE SEA, AND TWO LARGE GATES ... IN THE SIDES TOWARDS THE WOOD. WITHIN WERE FOURTEEN HOUSES, OR *BARABARAS* ... AS THEY ARE CALLED BY THE NATIVES. JUDGING FROM THE QUANTITY OF DRIED FISH, AND OTHER SORTS OF PROVISION, AND THE NUMEROUS EMPTY BOXES AND DOMESTIC IMPLEMENTS WHICH WE FOUND, IT MUST HAVE CONTAINED AT LEAST EIGHT HUNDRED MALE INHABITANTS."

– LISYANSKY (1814)

The fortification, immune to gunfire, armed with European-supplied cannon and filled with 800 warriors, must have been a challenging prospect indeed for the Russian reprisal fleet on their return to Sitka in 1804 (Lisyansky was the commander of the sloop-of-war *Neva*.) Furthermore, the new fortification had been located at the mouth of the Indian River, which had extensive shallows stretching out into the bay, making approach by Russian ships extremely difficult.

First contact between the Russian force, which consisted of four small Russian warships manned by 150 Russian fur traders, supported by up to 500 Aleuts manning their native kayaks, came on September 29, 1804. The Russians landed some distance from the Tlingit fortification, and initially attempted to negotiate a peaceful solution. Their efforts were rejected, and battle opened shortly after when the Russians spotted a group of Tlingit warriors transporting gunpowder by canoe back to the fort. The Russians opened fire and hit the canoes, killing all the powder-gathering party in a huge explosion when the gunpowder detonated.

On October 1, the attack on the Tlingit fortification began in earnest. Having been towed up the shallows by smaller craft, the *Neva* unloaded an artillery detachment onto the beach

▲ A large Russian naval expedition arrives by boat at Sitka in 1804 under the command of Aleksandr Baranov, the first Russian governor of Alaska. The Russians faced large numbers of Tlingit warriors and had to tackle Native American fortifications whose walls could even withstand naval gunfire.

area to fire on the fort, while the Aleut made a direct assault on the walls. Both of these efforts came to nothing, the fortification walls shrugging off the Russian shot while the Aleuts suffered heavy casualties from Tlingit fire and were forced to retreat back to their kayaks. The Tlingit followed up with a counter-attack, trapping the Aleuts and accompanying Russians in an action that left a dozen of the allied force dead, and several Russian artillery pieces abandoned on the beach.

The second day saw a change of Russian strategy. The commander of the expedition, Alexandr Baranov, had been wounded in the previous day's engagement, so Lisyansky took over. Rather than attempt another costly land attack, Lisyansky opted for three days of naval bombardment against the fortification. Although the shots did not initially penetrate the Tlingit defenses, they did start to wear them down and also prevent the Tlingit from conducting operations of their own.

Furthermore, the Tlingit were starting to run out of gunpowder, and they eventually decided simply to abandon the fortification, slipping into the woods under cover of darkness. When the Russians finally entered the fortification, they found that the Tlingit had massacred their own infants and dogs, to prevent their noise giving them away. The Russians then burnt the fortification to the ground.

The battle at Sitka is of a rather different kind to

▲ Alexandr Andreyevich Baranov (1746–1819), the Russian trader who rose to become the head of the Russian–American Company and a force against the Indians of the Pacific Northwest.

▲ Members of the Tlingit tribe in Klukwan village circa 1895, surrounded by totemic carvings. The Tlingit owed much of their culture to Asiatic European origins, hence the oriental allusions in their clothing.

many we having encountered in this book. It proved the strength of the Northwest Indian defenses against even a modern naval force, while also illustrating their vulnerability to a prolonged action. Here was the Achilles heel of subsistence communities. While they could be ferocious in the short-term, long-term needs would always limit their ability to prosecute war.

Glossary

ad hoc Formed or done strictly for a particular purpose.
artillery Large-caliber guns.
ascertain To make sure of something.
assimilation The absorption and integration of people or culture into a wider society or culture.
auxiliary A person or thing giving additional help and support.
barricade An improvised barrier meant to prevent or delay opposing troops from moving forward.
bombardment A continuous attack with bombs or other missiles.
burgeoning Beginning to grow rapidly; flourishing
buttressed Providing a structure with projecting supports built against its walls.
caustic Able to burn or corrode organic tissue through chemical action.
column A line of people moving in the same direction.
connotation An idea or feeling invoked by a word in addition to its literal meaning.
dehumanize To deprive someone of positive human qualities.
depredation The act of attacking or plundering.
detachment A group of troops sent away on a separate mission.
dichotomous Exhibiting or characterized by the division between two things that are opposed or entirely different.
fortification A defensive wall or reinforcement built to strengthen a location against attacks.
impregnable Unable to be broken into or destroyed.
ingenuity The quality of being clever and inventive.
knap To shape a piece of stone by striking it to make weapons or tools.
massacre The indiscriminate slaughter of people.
mediator A person who attempts to resolve a conflict between other people or groups; a go-between.
Mexican-American War An armed conflict that took place between Mexico and the United States from 1846 to 1848, following the U.S. annexation of Texas and resulting in the Rio Grande being recognized as the border between the countries.
Mexican War of Independence An armed conflict between Mexico and Spain from 1810 to 1821, resulting in Mexico's independence from Spain.
mold A hollow container used to give shape to molten or hot liquid material as it hardens while cooling.

neophyte A new convert to a religion.

obsidian A hard, dark, glasslike volcanic rock.

ostentatious Characterized by vulgar or pretentious display intended to attract notice.

palisades Long, pointed stakes that are placed next to each other to form a defensive barrier.

percussion cap A small amount of explosive powder contained in metal or paper that is exploded by striking.

provision Supply of food, drink, or equipment.

putrefaction The process of decay or rotting in organic matter, such as a body. Military observation of a region to locate an enemy or determine strategic features.

Russian-American Company A Russian state-sponsored company intended to establish new settlements in Alaska and California, conduct trade with the natives, and expand colonization efforts. It existed from 1799 to 1881.

savanna A grassy plain with few trees.

scalping Cutting off the skin and hair on a portion of the crown of a person's head after killing them, as a trophy.

shard A piece of broken rock, metal, or glass with sharp edges.

sinew A piece of tough fibrous tissue in the body, such as a tendon or ligament.

slat A thin, narrow piece of wood or other material that is designed to overlap or fit into each other.

static Lacking in movement, action, or change.

Further Reading

Confer, Clarissa, Andrae Marak, and Laura Tuennerman, ed. *Transnational Indians in the North American West* (Connecting the Greater West). College Station, TX: Texas A&M University Press, 2015.

Cothran, Boyd. *Remembering the Modoc War: Redemptive Violence and the Making of American Innocence* (First Peoples: New Directions in Indigenous Studies). Chapel Hill: University of North Carolina Press, 2014.

Kan, Sergei, ed. *Sharing Our Knowledge: The Tlingit and Their Coastal Neighbors.* Lincoln, NE: University of Nebraska Press, 2015.

Kuiper, Kathleen, ed. *Indigenous Peoples of the Arctic, Subarctic, and Northwest Coast* (Native American Tribes). New York: Britannica Educational Publishing and Rosen Educational Services, 2012.

Kuiper, Kathleen, ed. *Native Americans of California, the Great Basin, and the Southwest* (Native American Tribes). New York: Britannica Educational Publishing and Rosen Educational Services, 2012.

Linde, Barbara M. *Native Americans in Early North American* (American History). New York: Lucent Press, 2017.

Lobo, Susan, Steve Talbot, and Traci L. Morris. *Native American Voices: A Reader.* Abingdon, UK: Routledge, 2016.

Lowenstein, Tom and Piers Vitebsky. *Native American Myths and Beliefs* (World Mythologies). New York: The Rosen Publishing Group, 2012.

McNab, Chris. *Native American Warriors: 1500 CE-1890 CE.* New York, NY: Chartwell Books, 2016.

Wakim Dennis, Yvonne, Arlene B. Hirschfelder, and Shannon Rothenberger Flynn. *Native American Almanac: More Than 50,000 Years of the Cultures and Histories of Indigenous Peoples.* Canton, MI: Visible Ink Press, 2016.

Websites

The Invasion of America: How the United States Took Over an Eighth of the World
http://invasionofamerica.ehistory.org
This interactive map offers a look at the progression of colonialism and westward expansion through Native American territories.

National Museum of the American Indian Collections Search
http://www.nmai.si.edu/searchcollections/home.aspx
The Smithsonian National Museum of the American Indian's online collection contains images of a vast array of Indian artifacts and art, both contemporary and historical. The collection is searchable by culture, region, artist, and object specifications, and contains detailed information on the objects' history and material qualities.

Native American Masks of the Northwest Coast and Alaska
http://natural-history.uoregon.edu/collections/web-galleries/native-american-masks-northwest-coast-and-alaska
This gallery from the University of Oregon contains images of a variety of masks created by tribes in the Northwest and Canada, with a brief explanation of their origin and place in the culture.

INDEX

A
Alaska, 5, 18, 31, 39
ambush, 11, 15, 26, 30, 32
armor, types of, 9, 35, 36

B
Bannock tribe, 7, 11
Baranov, Alexandr, 42
battle tactics, 25
Bear Hunter, 12
Bear River, Battle of, 12, 21
blades, 23
bows, types of, 20–21, 23

C
California, 5, 6, 7, 8, 9, 11, 14, 15, 19, 20, 24, 25, 31
Canada, 5
Canby, Edward, 15
children, killing of, 10, 11, 28, 29, 30
Christianity, 7, 8
clubs, 19, 23, 30
Colorado, 24
Columbia River, 5
Conder, Josiah, 27
Conner, Patrick, 11–12
counting coup, 26
Cox, Jacob D., 16–18
Crook, George, 14

F
firearms, availability of to Indians, 24–25
formal warfare, methods of, 25–26
fortifications, types of, 24, 38–39
Franciscans, 6
Fraser River, 5

G
geographic boundaries, of West Coast and Plateau/Basin Indians, 5
Ghost Dance, 15
gold, 9–10, 11
Grant, Ulysses S., 16
guerilla warfare, methods of, 26–28

H
hunting techniques, 27

J
Jarboe, Walter, 10
Joint Special Committee on the Mendocino Indian War, 11

K
Kientopos, "Captain Jack," 15
Klamath tribe, 15
Kumeyaay tribe, 8

M
Mexican-American War of 1846–48, 9
Mexicans, 6, 7, 9
Mexican War of Independence, 9
missionaries, 6, 9
Miwok tribe, 7, 9
Modoc tribe, 7, 14–16
Modoc War, 14–16
Mohave tribe, 9
Mono tribe, 7, 19
mules, 14

O
Oregon, 11, 14, 38

P
Pacific Northwest Indians, lifestyle of, 31–32, 34–36, 38–39, 42–43
Paiute tribes, 7, 11, 14, 30
Peace Policy, 16, 18
poisons, 19

R
raiding, 9, 11, 12, 24, 26, 32, 35
railroad, 17, 18
reservations, establishment of, 18
Rocky Mountains, 5, 11, 20
Round Valley Reservation, 10
Russians, 6, 39, 42–43

S
San Joaquin Valley, 9
scalping, 25, 26, 29, 30
seaborne warfare, 32, 34, 36
Sherman, William Tecumseh, 16
Shoshone, 7, 11, 12, 21
    treaty with United States, 13
Sierra Nevada, 5, 10
Sitka Sound, Battle of, 39, 42–43
"Snake War," 14
Spanish, 6, 7, 8–11
spears, 19, 23, 35, 38

T
terror tactics, 28–30
Turner, George, 5

U
United States
    conflicts with Indian tribes, 6, 11–12, 14–15
    treaty with Shoshone, 13

W
weapons, types of, 19–21, 23
Weller, John, 10
women, killing of, 10, 11, 30

Y
Yavapai tribe, 19
Yokut tribe, 7, 9
Yuki tribe, 7, 10, 25